Sister Anne's Hands

MARYBETH LORBIECKI ✦ illustrated by K. WENDY POPP

DIAL BOOKS FOR YOUNG READERS 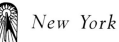 New York

Published by Dial Books for Young Readers
A member of Penguin Putnam Inc.
375 Hudson Street
New York, New York 10014

Designed by Ann Finnell
Printed in Hong Kong on acid-free paper
First Edition
5 7 9 10 8 6 4

Library of Congress Cataloging in Publication Data
Lorbiecki, Marybeth.
Sister Anne's hands/Marybeth Lorbiecki;
illustrated by K. Wendy Popp.—1st ed.
p.   cm.
Summary: Seven-year-old Anna has her first encounter with racism in the 1960's
when an African-American nun comes to teach at her parochial school.
ISBN 0-8037-2038-6 (trade).—ISBN 0-8037-2039-4 (lib. bdg.)
[1. Race relations—Fiction. 2. Schools—Fiction.
3. Afro-Americans—Fiction.] I. Popp, K. Wendy, ill. II. Title.
PZ7.L8766Si   1998 [Fic]—dc21   97-26671   CIP   AC

✧

The art is rendered in pastels.

To Sr. Anne Thompson and all dedicated and inspiring teachers.
With special thanks to Muriel Dubois; Jill Anderson;
my husband, David; my sister, Jean; and my brother, John.

M L

✧

For Nonna and those who teach and celebrate our common humanity.

I would like to acknowledge Principal Susan Luther of Central School; the faculty, particularly Caroline Clyne,
Jill Charwinsky, and Ms. Quitman; and the parents of the children whose faces may or may not be represented here,
for integrating my drawing process and need for life models into their classes as an educational experience.
I thank St. Augustine's and the Larchmont Library for their faith and permission to use their premises
for the settings of this imagery. My gratitude to my daughter, Zoe, and our friend Ester,
whose generous spirit and inner beauty emanate from the faces of Anna and Sister Anne.
And most particularly, to the children, Zoe's classmates and friends,
who modeled for me with eagerness and trust, a heartfelt thank you.
Finally, my admiration to author Marybeth Lorbiecki for the courage to focus on a very poignant topic
addressed to children, and to Dial for inviting me into such a rewarding project.

K W P

The summer I turned seven, flowers had power, peace signs were in, and we watched *The Ed Sullivan Show* every Sunday night. That's the summer word went around that a new teacher had come to town.

One night, after we'd been put to bed, Mom said in a whisper, "She'll be Anna's teacher."

And Dad replied, "I don't know how a woman of her color is going to survive."

Of her color? I wondered. What color could she be? Purple? Green? Orange? That night my dreams were full of teachers as colorful as birds.

Finally, the day came when I walked down the hall to my new room and saw her. She had on a black dress and veil like all the other nuns, but her skin was darker than any person's I'd ever known.

"And who are you, child?" she said with sparkles in her voice.

"Anna Zabrocky," I answered, seeing she had a space between her teeth just like me.

"Mighty fine freckles you have," she said, smiling widely. "Anyone kissed by angels as much as you, must have wings sprouting for sure."

Well, let me tell you, no one had ever connected *me* with angels before. I was the one they sent to the hall for talking in class or to the principal for mouthing off.

When she reached out to touch my cheek, I dodged her hand as if it were hot. It was puppy brown with white lacy moons for nails. And palm side up, it was pink with dark lines. A light pretty pink like an evening dress for Barbie. I tried not to stare.

She didn't seem to notice. "Welcome to the second grade. I'm Sister Anne."

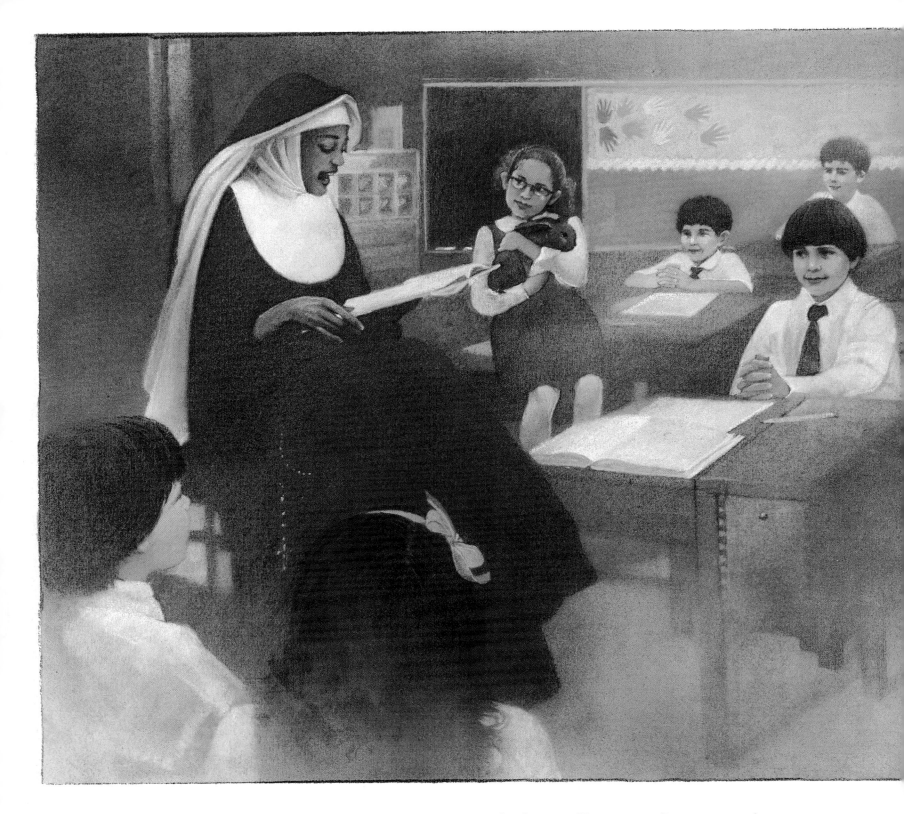

That day, to start class, Sister Anne had us tell some of our very best
jokes, even the nun ones like "What's black and white, and black and white,
and black and white? . . . A nun rolling down the stairs."

And when she read to us at story time, she did all the voices, low or high or grunting.

Then she had us counting the buttons on our clothes, pencils in our desks, and teeth in our heads.

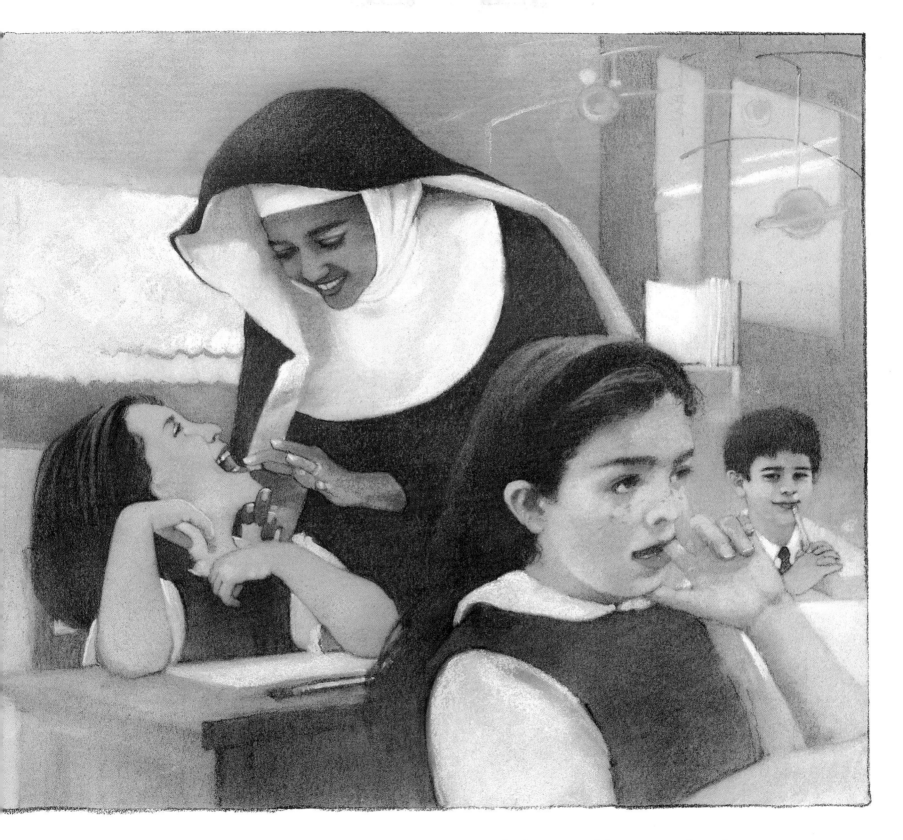

After all that adding and subtracting, we ended up toothless, pencil-rich,
and with buttons on our underwear. I'd never had so much fun at school!

But after lunch, a paper airplane sailed past Sister's head and hit the blackboard—WHOOSH.

There was a note written on the wings. Sister Anne read it out loud:
"Roses are red,
Violets are blue.
Don't let Sister Anne
get any black on you."
A few giggles rippled across the room. Sister's face froze like a tongue on an icy post.

"This is funny?" she asked us softly.

We didn't say a thing. I felt as guilty as if I'd made the airplane.

"I'll need some quiet time to think about this, if you know what I mean."

We did. You could have heard a butterfly sigh for the rest of that day. We went home with plenty on our minds.

That night in my bed, all I could see was Sister Anne's hand as she reached out to me.

The next morning, we all slunk into the classroom, and we were shocked at what we saw. Sister Anne had plastered the room with pictures of black people, poor or dying, some hanging from trees, others shot and bleeding.

We saw signs over water fountains saying "Whites Only," and people marching with posters: "Go Back to Africa."

None of us knew what to say.

"*These* are the colors of hatred," Sister Anne said. "Do you know how they feel? In some places if you had to go to the bathroom, and the only toilet not being used was the one for colored people, you'd have to hold it or go behind a tree." That had us squirming in our seats.

Then she seemed to warm up to us a little. "One thing you're going to learn is that some folks have their hearts wide open, and others are tight as a fist. The tighter they are, the more dangerous.

"For me, I'd rather open my door enough to let everyone in than risk slamming it shut on God's big toe."

All of a sudden I could see this big toenail hanging out of the clouds, and I wanted to laugh. It was clear. Sister Anne was giving us another chance.

"Now," she said, "I was sent here to teach, and that's what I'm going to do."

And she did. Some kids were pulled from her class by their parents, but we didn't miss them much.

Sister Anne taught us to write and paint and garden.

She had us singing and clapping and stomping our feet while learning our
two plus twelve and six minus three.

She took us to the library to visit islands in the ocean and countries across the sea. She taught us about people we'd never heard of before, like Phillis Wheatley, Matthew Henson, and Sojourner Truth.

There was this minister she liked too, Dr. Martin Luther King, who was
sometimes on the television news. She said he was trying to help people of
all different colors get along.

The year zoomed past so fast, I could hardly believe it.

On the last day of school, Sister Anne gave us the bad news: She wouldn't be coming back. She had been transferred to a school in Chicago.

When it came time to say good-bye, I stuck around till everyone else had gone. Then I pulled out a card I'd made for her. Inside were two hands—one white with little orange polka dots and the other filled with browns and pinks and whites.

Sister Anne just stared at the card for a long time. She didn't say anything, but her eyes got kinda watery.

Finally, she smiled and touched my face. "Looks like my little Anna Angel is learning how to use her wings."

I never heard what happened to Sister Anne after she left for Chicago. But I do know what happened to me. Now whenever I draw someone's hands—or big toes—I fill them in with browns and pinks and whites, reds and yellows and blues, polka dots, circles, and stripes.